Al volante / At the Wheel

Quiero conducir una quitanieves

I Want to Drive a Snowplow

Henry Abbot

traducido por / translated by

Eida de la Vega

ilustrado por / illustrated by

Aurora Aguilera

PowerKiDS
press.

New York

Published in 2017 by The Rosen Publishing Group, Inc.
29 East 21st Street, New York, NY 10010

First Edition

Translator: Eida de la Vega
Editorial Director, Spanish: Nathalie Beullens-Maoui
Editor, English: Theresa Morlock
Book Design: Michael Flynn
Illustrator: Aurora Aguilera

Cataloging-in-Publication Data

Names: Abbot, Henry, author.
Title: I want to drive a snowplow = Quiero conducir una quitanieves / Henry Abbot.
Description: New York : PowerKids Press, [2017] | Series: At the wheel = Al volante | Includes index.
Identifiers: ISBN 9781499429404 (library bound book)
Subjects: LCSH: Snowplows–Juvenile literature.
Classification: LCC TD868 .A23 2017 | DDC 625.7/63–dc23

Manufactured in the United States of America

CPSIA Compliance Information: Batch #BW17PK: For Further Information contact Rosen Publishing, New York, New York at 1-800-237-9932

Contenido

Contents

Me gustaría conducir una quitanieves. ¿Cómo sería?

I want to drive a snowplow. What would it be like?

5

6

Nevó mucho durante la noche. Cuando me despierto, el pueblo está cubierto de nieve.

It snowed a lot overnight. When I wake up, the town is covered in snow.

8

¡Es hora de que la quitanieves haga su trabajo! Voy a conducirla hoy.

It's time for the snowplow to get to work! I'm going to drive it today.

9

Una quitanieves es un camión grande. Tiene una pala en el frente.

A snowplow is a big truck.

It has a plow in front.

Tengo que subir unos escalones para poder entrar a la cabina.

I have to climb stairs to get in the snowplow.

¡Es así de grande!

That's how big it is!

13

Echo a andar la quitanieves.

Entonces salgo a la calle.

I turn on the snowplow.

Then I pull it out on to the street.

14

15

La quitanieves tiene ruedas grandes y gruesas. Se mueven con facilidad sobre la nieve y el hielo.

The snowplow has big, thick wheels. They easily roll over snow and ice.

16

Presiono un botón para bajar la pala.

La pala empuja la nieve fuera del camino.

I push a button to lower the plow.

It pushes snow out of the way.

Presiono otro botón.

La pala recoge la nieve del suelo. ¡Vaya!

I push another button.

The plow scoops the snow off the ground. Wow!

21

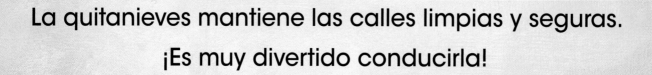

La quitanieves mantiene las calles limpias y seguras.
¡Es muy divertido conducirla!

My snowplow makes the streets clear and safe.
It's fun to drive a snowplow!

23

Palabras que debes aprender
Words to Know

(la) pala
plow

(la) nieve
snow

(las) ruedas
wheels

Índice / Index